A Cat With Three Tales
by Karen Rieser

©Karen Rieser 2013

ISBN: 978-1-937260-93-4

Published in the U.S.A.

Published by Sleepytown Press

Dedication

Max's story is being told to honor all the men and women who spend countless hours working to rescue, foster, and care for animals in need.

In addition I want to thank
Blackjack, Lassie, Sneakers, Fred, Sarah, Silver and Pearl, my feline companions, who have loved and cared for me over my lifetime.

Thank You to Laurie Dalton for contributing the photos.

Chapter 1

As mother's prickly tongue stroked every inch of his new-born body he fumbled his way through her soft fur to find a source of sweet milk. Push, push, push, he kneaded his mother's belly. Life giving nourishment filled his stomach, as an unexpected purring sound seemed to erupt from his chest. There were others, warm, and purring next to him. Sleep soon came over this litter of newborn gray and black tabby kittens. It had been quite a long day, for mom, birthing this litter of four. For the kittens, coming into this world had not been an easy task. But at last, warmth, full tummies, and sweet sleep were theirs.

This incredible miracle had gone on unnoticed in the back of Madeline's closet, right on top of her once favorite sweat-shirt and a pile of forgotten socks. It would be a couple of days before Madeline heard their cries and found this contented family. With great excitement she ran to tell her mother and father. Mom and Dad, however, did not greet this news with the same enthusiasm. The kittens could stay with their mother until they were six weeks old and would then have to be given away. Madeline's heart ached as she accepted her parent's decision.

Madeline decided that as long as Sapphire's kittens stayed with her they would have a comfortable life. A box from the local grocery store was turned into an elegant bed. This feline family slept on a pillow covered with a fluffy bath towel, one of Mom's best. Next to their box was a placemat for Sapphire's breakfast, lunch and dinner. If she were going to feed these kittens she would need to keep up her strength. Madeline gave her fancy canned cat food and served her warm milk with each meal. Purrs and warm eyes came from this loving abode.

Six weeks passed much too quickly. The family would take the litter, two males and two females, to Miss Lilly. Madeline had chosen to leave the kittens with Miss Lilly because for years Miss Lilly had found homes for all sorts of cats. As a matter of fact, Miss Lilly had let Madeline adopt Sapphire. The kittens would go to Miss Lilly's at the end of the week.

The weekend came too quickly. Their elegant home was loaded into the car. The kittens were falling all over one another crying for their mother who was back in Madeline's room. Madeline had a knot in her stomach as she carried the box through Miss Lilly's door and into the cat room. As usual Miss Lilly said all the right things and had a place prepared for the kittens. They got to keep their box, pillow and towel. There was milk and food waiting for them.

Madeline left quickly giving each kitten a hug, a kiss, and a wish for a good life.

Chapter 2

It was strangely quiet and uncomfortably cold without mom. The kittens snuggled together trying to find comfort. The days and nights seemed so long and empty. Slowly they learned to depend on each other for contentment. They ate together, chased, tumbled, ran every which way, and fell into a pile to sleep. Time passed.

Miss Lilly thought Madeline's kittens were lovely. She wanted people to see them as soon as possible. Within the week she took them to their first adoption event. Into a cat carrier they went. Some time later when the kittens emerged they were in the middle of a huge store with hundreds of eager eyes peering in at them. There was a lot of ooohing and ahing. Now and them they were picked up and pet.

Both the female kittens found homes that day. One went with a young girl and the other with twin boys. The male kittens watched as their siblings were carried off, tucked under coats to be kept warm, and smothered with kisses.

That night it was harder to keep warm and a bit lonely. Miss Lilly warmed their milk just like Madeline had, but it just wasn't the same. First, they had to learn to live without their mother and now without their sisters. The boys would have to get used to this, as they attended many more adoption events only to be brought back to Miss Lilly's. That was before Judith spotted them.

Judith was a striking woman of about 30. She had stopped by the adoption event on her way home from work. Her job as a computer analyst kept her very busy. She lived by herself in a very comfortable two-bedroom apartment, but was lonely. Judith thought a cat would be the perfect companion. A cat would sleep most of the day and entertain itself. When Judith got home the cat would be there to greet her and snuggle as they watched TV and slept.

Miss Lilly greeted Judith with a smile and a handshake. She carefully reviewed Judith's papers. Miss Lilly felt Judith would make a good adoptive parent for one of her cats. They walked around the room looking into each cage. Judith didn't want a kitten but she didn't want a cat that was too old either. One of Madeline's kittens seemed like they might fit the bill. They had grown in the weeks they had waited for a family but were still young.

Judith was thrilled when she peered into the cage marked male, friendly, twenty weeks old. She smiled and held each kitten. One was very frisky and the other a bit shy. Oh they are lovely she thought. She would take the frisky one. Oh, but the shy one, just look at those sweet eyes, I think he loves me. No, the frisky one will make me laugh….but those loving eyes. As one might expect both boys went home with Judith. She had fallen in love with them both and knew she had room in her heart and home for two very different black and gray tabby kittens.

Chapter 3

The frisky kitten became known as Squirrely as he jumped on the furniture as a squirrel jumps around a tree. Friday fit the shy kitten, as he was calm, casual, and cool.

Friday and Squirrely found Judith's apartment to be very comfortable. There were hardwood floors to slide on. The many potted plants held so many good smells. The plants of greatest interest were geraniums that lined the open edges of the balcony. Sometimes birds sat on their long branches and mice used them to rest and hide in. During the warm months there was a small table and chairs on the balcony. The chairs had lovely cushions to sleep on in the sun. Sometimes Judith joined them on the balcony with a cup of tea and the Kindle on which she read her newspaper. Those were very nice days. On other days the favorite sleeping spot was the over stuffed green corduroy couch that sat in front of the glass wall. Oh, the sun warmed that couch and their fur the whole daylong. Of course, when Judith came home and it was time for bed they all crawled into her queen size bed weaving themselves into one another and the down comforter.

Squirrely and Friday spent all their time inside. City life was too scary. Cars, trucks, taxis, buses, bicycles, busy children, grown ups walking fast and hungry homeless cats and dogs were all too much to have to worry about. They were very satisfied to observe this world from the windows or balcony; there was no need to actually experience it. For several years life was good for all concerned.

Then one-day life was not so good. Judith had been hugging and kissing them a lot. She had also been crying, leaving their fur wet after she had held them. As they groomed themselves the salt from her tears was definitely there. Boxes had been moved into the apartment and things were disappearing. One of the most disturbing changes was that all their geraniums were now lined up in a straight row on the balcony next door.

Judith had tried to explain to them that she was moving to California to a new and much better job. Sadly, she could not bring them with her. But Squirrely and Friday just had no idea what she was trying to tell them, they just knew life seemed different somehow.

Then that day came. Huddled in their cat carrier, they did not stop at the vet, but at Miss Lilly's front door. Judith handed the carrier to Miss Lilly. She took a minute to peer into the carrier, but it was too hard. Miss Lilly would take good care of them.

Why, oh why were they back. They just curled up together and waited.

Chapter 4

They waited, and waited, and waited. They were four years old now. They went from adoption event to adoption event. They must have watched fifty or more kittens be carried out the door to new homes. People hardly looked in their cage and when they did they heard: Oh, old ones or they must have a problem if no one wants them. Why, can't they read the sign that says: Brothers, well behaved, four years old.

Attending these events became a way of life for Squirrely and Friday. They had accompanied Miss Lilly every week-end for two years and never had an offer. Squirrely tried to remain hopeful but Friday lost all hope. Why bother, he thought, and he took to sleeping in his covered litter box where no one could see him. He no longer wanted to hear the disparaging remarks or be stared at.

Chapter 5

Friday had been dozing for some time when a large hand reached into his litter box and began to painfully pull at him. Oh, his shoulders and legs were being stretched beyond their limits. It hurt. Leave me alone! Just leave me alone!

Once out of his box and cage he felt the coolness of the air and squinted from the bright light. He was hanging from his shoulders as he was being pulled into a warm body. He sniffed. It had been such a long time since he had felt this sort of cuddling. Oh, she was stroking his back and massaging his ears and jaw. She had obviously done this before. What joy.

Friday immediately snuggled into her neck and held on tight. He did not want to leave as he yearned for comfort.

Could it be he had found a home? This promising thought began to fade as he realized something was not right. There was a lot of walking back and forth and a long sometimes-tense conversation with Miss Lilly.

This family definitely wanted him but they wanted him to-day. Miss Lilly had a very strict rule….a three day waiting period before you could take a cat home. She had to check with your vet and make sure you would be a good parent to her cat.

Miss Lilly watched, as Friday was being loved! Another young woman was trying to explain that they wanted to make sure the cat worked out for their aging parents before they left for their homes miles away. They promised if the cat did not work out they would bring it back. If the cat did work out he would never want for anything for the rest of his life.

Friday could tell Miss Lilly was thinking very hard. She always got those wrinkles in her forehead when she did. Miss Lilly looked from one woman to the other and back again. She knew Friday needed a home and perhaps living with an older couple would be just the thing for him. She decided she would take a chance.

As Friday was placed in the cat carrier things did not seem so very sweet. Yes, he was getting a new home but without Squirrely. Where was he going, how was he going to live, and it was so dark in the carrier. He bounced around as he was taken to the car. He was so anxious he began to choke and cough. A pair of green eyes appeared along with some soothing words. Friday took a deep breath and sat back. He could change nothing and just had to wait and see what was going to happen. He sat, and sat, and sat, this ride was taking forever.

Chapter 6

There was a lot of chatter and excitement in the car. Every-one was so pleased to have finally found a cat. They had driven for hours looking at cats. They had found plenty of kittens but they knew Mom and Dad would not want some frisky creature hanging from the curtains and needing con-stant care. The cats they did find either bit, came with kittens or did not appear friendly. With each inquiry they had been told they needed a vet recommendation and character refer-ences. They had no time for that. They needed to see the cat with Mom and Dad for several days before their visit ended. Dumping a cat and leaving would not have been fair to the cat or their parents.

After what seemed like forever the car slowed down, turned a corner and came to a stop. They were home and I guess Friday guessed he was too.

Chapter 7

The carrier and bags of cat supplies were pulled out of the car and brought into the kitchen. Mom and Dad were just sitting down to lunch. The kitchen doors were closed and Friday presented. To say this was a surprise was an understatement.
Friday just stood there paralyzed. He looked at them as they stared back at him.

"What are we going to do with a cat?" said Dad.

" Love him of course," the girls said.

Friday was worried, he didn't move. Mom and Dad looked at the cat, the cat looked at Mom and Dad, the silence was deafening.

Mom got up and began unpacking Friday's supplies. She poured his food into his bowl and put it in the mudroom. She also gave him a bowl of milk. Friday went to smell his lunch, but was too nervous to eat. He still had a knot in his stomach the size of a baseball. Next the litter box was set out. Friday just stared. There was no top, too bad because he wanted to crawl inside something and hide from all this newness.

It was decided. For now the cat would stay. Mom and Dad were pleased, but nervous about the new member of the family. Friday felt the same. It was decided that Friday would now be Max.

All was looking good. Friday had a new name, home, and family to love him. His dreams had come true, or had they. The family opened the kitchen doors for Max to explore his new home and he took off like a shot. He ran across the foyer, up the stairs (he had never used stairs before, but seemed to be good at them), down the hall, into a bedroom and under the bed. He was not seen for days.

Chapter 8

Max's stomach seemed to be getting the best of him. Except for his rumbling tummy, the house was very dark and quiet. He poked his head out from under the bed and sniffed. Now seemed as good a time as any to explore. He walked very cautiously across the room to the door. He sniffed. Coast was clear. As he made his way to the stairs he watched every corner. He bounded down the stairs, the foyer floor was cold as he crossed and found the kitchen. His bowl was still there full of kibbles and a fresh bowl of milk sat next to it.

Max ate and drank until that warm purr found its way to his chest. Content, he was ready to check out the rest of this house. It was a large house with many rooms and more stairs going to a basement. There were good smells down there and neat places to hide if he needed them. With dust on his whiskers he found his way back to the mudroom. A few more nibbles took the edge off his hunger. He curled up in the corner on a fallen jacket and fell asleep.

Chapter 9

The morning light coming from the backdoor window woke Max with its brightness and warmth. He stood and arched his back into a marvelous morning stretch. His front legs stretched out before him as the stretch rippled through his body to his toes. This was a good morning. His tummy was still full, he was rested and...oh no, voices were coming from the kitchen.

He poked his head out the doorway to see a man and woman eating their breakfast.

"Well there you are. It's about time you found your way around."

Max approached them cautiously. The woman put her worn hand down for Max to smell. She tried to touch his head and ears. Oh no, no touching. Max backed up but did not run away. Next the man put his hand down, sniff sniff. No attempt was made to touch him this time.

The woman walked over to his kibbles and arranged them in the bowl for him to eat. Max didn't know yet but this would become a loving habit he would share with his new Mom for the rest of her life. He ate a bit and lapped up some cool milk. It was now time to sit in the sun and groom, first the face, then the ears, and now the tummy. The three of them spent a lovely morning watching one another as he bathed and they read the New York Times. Max realized he was the only animal sharing the house with them and was feeling very safe. This might work out after all.

As the sun moved across the sky Max moved from room to room catching the sun in his fur. There were a lot of windows from which to check out the birds, chipmunks, and squirrels. Even though he no longer lived in the city he had no desire to go outside and confront these creatures, but he still had that feline interest in stalking them.

By the end of the day he rubbed on his Mom's legs to mark her as his. She arranged his kibbles for him; he ate and found a corner of her bed to sleep on. There was still no touching, that would come soon enough.

Chapter 10

As the days went on life continued to be just as comfortable as it had been that first day Max decided to join the family. Then that inevitable day came, the day he must visit the vet. One of the girls came to help out. He was put into his carrier and put into the car. Mom and Dad came with him. Well, he was not going to be sent away again and he was going to make that known. He began to yowl in protest and did not quit until he got to the vet.

The vet ran her hands over his body, looked in his eyes, ears, at his feet and listened to his heart and lungs. With a smile the vet announced she had found Max to be a robust specimen of a cat. Now Max could have told her that. Unfortunately there were a few shots, but Max dealt with that.

Back into the carrier and the car. Max was pretty sure he was going home, but was still going to make his displeasure known. He did so by giving a yowl fest all the way home. Once back in the house Max jumped out of the carrier and strolled into the living room for a bit of sun.

Although Max was content to be home, Mom and Dad were not happy. Putting Max through such an experience was not acceptable to them.

The girl, having had many pets herself, was aware of a vet that made house calls. Yes, it would be house calls for Max from then on.

Chapter 11

Max, Mom and Dad led a peaceful life. Quiet days, visitors here and there, and long naps. Max's food was ruffled everyday and there was always a bowl of fresh milk. He had come to enjoy being scratched on the head and behind the ears. He chose to never get up on the furniture as the sun always seemed to have a spot on the floor warmed for him. Life was good but then came Hoover.

Hoover, a big black lab, belonged to one of the girls. When she visited Mom and Dad he came with her. Max would never forget the first day they met. The front door opened and in bounded this galumph of a dog. He was huge, jet-black, mouth open, tongue hanging out. He ran into every room in about ten seconds.

Max immediately dove under the couch. Gads, his peaceful home had just been invaded. Dogs are so crude. They never keep anything to themselves. To be sure this dog was happy to be there and hopefully he would not be there for long.

Right away the daughter began to look for Max. She found him in no time. She begged him to come out. He had no intention of coming out while that crazy dog was behind her wiggling all over the place. This evidently was not to be Max's decision. The same hand that had reached into the kitty litter box so long ago was coming for him under the couch. She got him.

Oh drats! That dog was sniffing his face, belly and feet on his way up to the girl's loving hug. His tongue was so sloppy it was going to take Max hours to clean the dog stink off. He had forgotten what a good cuddler the girl was. He began to purr. And then it came, the get to know you time. She lowered Max to the floor for Hoover to sniff, and sniff he did. Once he was finished, Hoover gave out a juicy sneeze from all the cat fur he had inhaled and waltzed off to find his own patch of sun to curl up in.

Max just stood there paralyzed from all the activity. Once he regained his composure he found a spot of sun, which happened to be next to Hoover, the sun hog. He began the task of grooming. This was going to take a while.

Hoover did not pay much attention to Max. Maybe this wasn't going to be so bad after all. Once Max had cleaned his head and paws he decided he would nap for a while. Humm, a nice warm, body next to him. Why not. Max curled up against Hoover's side. Hoover lifted his head, looked at Max, sighed, and lay back down. Oh, what a marvelous nap. From that point on Max and Hoover were gentle companions whenever he visited.

Chapter 12

Max so enjoyed his pleasant days with Mom and Dad. End-less sun, ruffled food, newspapers to be read, life was so very good.

One day all three girls came to visit. Their activities were disturbing. A great many things were being carried out of the house and nothing was coming back in. Mom and Dad seemed upset, Max could feel it and if they were upset he was upset.

This went on for days. Then the boxes came in. Oh, he re-membered the boxes. The last time boxes took over his space he lost his home. Could this be happening again. All sorts of things were going into the boxes. Max's stomach hurt. Each day brought a greater ache; he could not keep his food down. He did not want anyone seeing him get sick so he ran behind boxes or in the basement. He was always found. They sent for the vet.

Max welcomed the vet's gentle touch and soothing voice. It was decided that Max had a nervous stomach. She left some powder to sprinkle onto his food. This made Max's tummy feel better, but not his heart. He was very, very worried. He sensed Mom and Dad were worried also and tried to put on a brave face.

The boxes kept being filled. The house was looking empty. Then it happened. Max was put into his carrier and taken to the car. Off he went with one of the girls and Mom at the wheel. Max yowled without really knowing why. Oh the pain in his heart. After some time he was worn out and fell asleep. When he woke up it was dark, quiet, and did not smell like anywhere he had been before.

Max waited for what seemed like hours. He began to hear people moving around. They seemed far away. Slowly, their voices and the noise got louder and louder. Bump, bang, Ugh! Ugh! The sounds went on for some time. He began to recognize some of the voices. Oh, Mom and Dad were there. He was still with them. Someone picked up his carrier and carried it into another room that seemed sunny and warm but the smell was not right. The top of his carrier was removed.

Max stayed still. Slowly he stretched his neck to take a peek. There were boxes everywhere. The room was small. One of the walls was a large window that went all the way to the floor. Mom and Dad began to coax him out of his crate. Slowly one foot at a time he stepped out onto the soft carpet. His eyes squinted from the sunlight. Once he was comfortable he peeked around a box.

Max crouched, made his back feet dance, and off he went… right for the window. Bam-slam his face flattened against the window. A chipmunk had been looking in from outside. Max surveyed the patio…where did that varmint go. You better stay off this patio, the mighty Max has arrived. The entire room full of people, all of whom had been holding their breath, began to roar with laughter.

To Max's satisfaction the boxes were being unpacked, the furniture from his other home was there and so were Mom and Dad. Soon the girls left and life was quiet again. The only difference was that Max sensed Mom and Dad did not seem to be as happy as they once were. Lots of things were different. The apartment was smaller than the house, but the windows were great....they went all the way to the floor in each room. The beds were new, but still good to hide under. Newspapers were still read, but meals were not eaten in the apartment as much. Dad used to watch the door. Watch out for Max he would say. Max didn't want to go out in the hallway…that was scary. There were strange people out there on motorized carts, in wheel chairs and walking. The apartment was his new home; it would be fine as long as Mom and Dad were with him most of the time.

Chapter 13

Max spent much of his time watching for chipmunks. There was quite a community set up in the bushes. As with his old house he followed the sun during the day. Sometimes the windows were opened so he could sniff at the fresh air. Hoover had found his new home and visited often. To his surprise it wasn't bad living there. Life was peaceful, until one afternoon it arrived, the vacuum.

Once a week the apartment was cleaned. People went into every room. Things were scrubbed, dishes were rattled, and towels and beds changed. Yes, he once again had to dive under the bed and hide from these intrusive humans. But worst of all was the giant sucking machine. It went everywhere and made so much noise. Why it was even shoved under the bed right at him. This was more than Max could bear. He had to make a break for it. He shot out from under the bed and made a beeline for Dad's bed. The peace lasted for only a few minutes before it was back again. Another break for it, and a dive under the living room buffet. Slam, the door was closed and silence once again.

Max lived through this experience every week. Somehow it always seemed new. Dad would get upset and watch the door so he wouldn't escape. He just didn't understand that for the most part Max was pleased with his life with Mom and Dad and would never leave them.

Chapter 14

On one of Hoover's visits he brought a marvelous toy, the fabulous cat dancer. It was really a simple toy. A piece of piano wire with bits of cardboard attached to each end. Oh, did Max love to chase that cardboard. He would leap into the air like a mighty feline, roll over on his back and kick at the cardboard beast. Chase, chase and chase....it was wild. Best of all his people cheered for him. He would play with the cat dancer for hours if they would let him.

Chapter 15

Over time Max began to notice small changes in his Mom and Dad. They could not move as fast, they slept more, and they did not go out as much. Max didn't mind this, as he loved spending time with them. The three of them would talk, play with the cat dancer, and he had his meals with the usual riffling from Mom.

One day Dad disappeared for a long time. Max didn't know it, but his dad was in the hospital after a fall. He stayed and kept Mom company. Max followed her everywhere. He slept with her, sat in the bathroom as she bathed, he liked the way the steam fluffed his fur, watched her cook, and enjoyed some TV.

Max had been keeping a good eye on mom all day when something very odd happened. She kept falling to the floor. She had never done this before. He meowed and meowed. Mom pushed the special button on her necklace and a lot of people came to her. They pushed Max out of the way with their feet. This just would not do. Max kept charging in to help mom. He yowled and paced. This wasn't right, it wasn't right. To Max's horror, they carried mom out of the apartment and the door shut behind her.

He was alone. It was dark, quiet and scary. People had taken him away before but his people had never been taken away. He waited in the quiet darkness for hours before he fell asleep.

When the sun came up Max didn't feel the usual joy in the warmth of a new day. He was still alone, it was still quiet, and it was still very scary, very scary. Late in the day Veronica came in to feed him. She did the shopping and laundry for Mom and Dad and was a nice enough person, but she never had pets or kind words for him. For days Veronica came into feed him. There was no ruffling of his food and no cat dancing. He waited and waited day after day.

Finally, Dad came home. Oh, Dad was delighted to see Max and Max was purr...fectly thrilled to see his Dad. Max would not leave his side, they just sat there and stared at each other. Dad kept the cat dancer by his chair and they played from time to time, but he did not ruffle his food.

Max was relieved to have Dad back, but he was so different. He could not walk anymore without a walker and he rode everywhere on a scooter. Dad was so slow and seemed sad. This worried Max very much. His tummy began to hurt again, he began to get sick and his skin itched all over. Dad called the vet who came right away. He got more medicine, which made him relax a bit.

Chapter 16

Finally, Mom came home. What had happened? She was in a wheelchair and needed people with her all the time. Oh, Max did not know if he liked so many people in his apartment. He would need to keep an eye on Mom. Max learned how to move around the wheelchair and stood guard as long as Mom was awake. When she was asleep he slept next to her. Mom seemed to like this as there was always a hand on his back, which made him purr.

Mom was never able to feed him again, but Dad got a fancy new tray with a handle that held his food and water. Dad could bend over and pick it up, fill his bowls and return his food to the ground. Max worried. He would never leave his Mom and Dad even if they couldn't feed him.

Life went on like this for quite a while. People came and went. They took care of all his Mom's needs and some of Dad's. Max stood guard, no one could make a move without his approval. He had had to swat Veronica a couple of times when she got too close to Mom. He also swatted Mary when she hurt Dad putting his socks on. Day after day his keen eyes protected the Mom and Dad he loved so deeply. They were never going to have to leave him again, never, he would work hard to see to it.

Chapter 17

Unfortunately, despite Max's diligence Mom did leave. This time she said a long good bye. Oh, his tummy was hurting so much or was it his heart. He just knew he would not see her again and he was right.

Dad came home, but left each day for a week. The girls were all there. Oh his heart ached so.

One day before Dad left he told Max that his Mom had said Max had been visiting her at night. If one's heart could send its love Max knew she had been right. His body had not been there, but his love and spirit would always be with her. That day Mom went to heaven.

The family returned and stayed together for some days. Slowly one by one they left. Dad looked at Max. Max looked at Dad. It was going to just be the boys from now on. They would miss Mom, but they were going to be strong and care for one another and that is just what they did.

Dad would not let anyone else feed Max. His new food carrier made that possible. Max would rub on Dad's legs as he lowered the food. He would purr and Dad would watch him eat. When it was time for Dad to eat, Max would watch him from a sunny spot on the floor. Everyday he groomed himself as dad had his breakfast. There would be a long warm nap after lunch as Max slept next to Dad. As with Mom there was always a warm hand at his side. Dinner was the most fun as Dad had taken to having ice cream for dinner and sometimes he got to lick the bowl. Dad went to bed early these days so Max got a very long nightly rest. He would watch the door when he wasn't sleeping, grooming, but mostly slept as he stayed by Dad's side.

As before, Max and Dad would have long talks, they liked to listen to music, play with the cat dancer (oh he never got tired of that), and rest. So many stories were told, Max was a good listener. The girls came and went. Sometimes Hoover came to visit, but then he went to the same place as Mom. Max didn't see him again. He felt his world getting smaller and smaller. It really didn't matter as long as he had his sunny spots, Dad, and the cat dancer. After a while life seemed almost good again and then came the horrible night.

Chapter 18

Max and Dad were right in the middle of their nightly rest. Dad sat up, the bed began to shake, Dad was crying. Just like Mom he pushed the magic button. People again, so many people. This time he wasn't going to let them take Dad away.

Dad sat on the edge of the bed and waited. Max stayed on the bed and paced. People tried to touch Dad, Max swatted them. Dad told them to leave Max alone and they did, but that did not keep him from swatting. Even though Max yowled, paced and swatted Dad was taken away.

There he was again in the quiet darkness without his Dad. He would wait again, but this time he yowled until he fell asleep.

It seemed like forever before someone came for him. Veronica feed him, cleaned his litter box, but no cat dancer. The girls came again . This could not be good. Dad was gone. Oh he could hardly stand this. He had really done his best to keep Dad here.

Chapter 19

The day finally came when Dad returned. Oh no...he was in a wheelchair. Now Dad had many people taking care of him. Dad was worried because he could not protect Max from the vacuum, the open door, feed him, play with the cat dancer.... he could not do anything. Dad cried as he talked to Max. He loved Max. No problem, Max loved Dad.

"Oh Max," Dad said, "you are my best and only friend. What do you make of an old man whose only friend is a cat." Dad tried to laugh. "Yes my only friend is a cat, but he is a very good cat. I love you Max. I love you so much I must send you away."

Dad broke into a flood of tears.

" You took such good care of me now I must take good care of you and let you go live with one of the girls. Oh Max, oh Max."

Tears flowed, hands shook, the last cat dance and then that awful moment of being lowered into the cat carrier. A quick exit was made as the pain was intense. Dad was crying, the girl was crying, and Max was yowling. In the hallway doors opened to see what all the commotion was about, but no one returned him to Dad. Why, why, oh why.

Chapter 20

Once again the cat carrier opened and Max had a new home. He hid for a while, but decided he'd better explore as he was very hungry. He cautiously climbed the stairs. Who was that sitting up there looking down on him. He appeared to be a small handsome cat. Max was curious. He approached cautiously. They gently sniffed noses. Max decided to give him a quick swat. He walked on into the kitchen. What had he just passed...dogs????? Humm. One didn't move, but the big black one came right up to smell him. Max swatted again only to have his paw end up under this dog's great lapping tongue. Gross, this canine was licking him all over and wagging his tail at the same time. Oh no, another goofy dog.

The girl watched this welcome and smiled.

"You're going to be fine, Max."

Would he be fine. When everyone was at work and all the other beasts were sleeping and Max sat in the window. It was a good window. He could see into the trees, down the driveway, and up the street. He would wait there for as long as it took for his Dad to come and find him.

And so, Max still sits, waiting for and loving his Mom and Dad. He watches as the flowers bloom, as the temperature rises, as the leaves turn colors and as the snow flies. As long as it takes.

Sadly in September, Max's Dad joined Mom and Hoover in heaven, but Max still waits. In the meantime he is loved and cared for by Mom and Dad's daughter. He will never be alone and someday he too will join Mom and Dad in heaven.

Epilogue

Today, Max is living very happily in Maryland. His food is ruffled by the girl, he sleeps with the dogs when the girl and her husband are at work and pretty much runs the house.

To the girls, Max is the angel that took their parents through the last stages of their lives. He brought them companionship, love, amusement and a sense of purpose. Should we all be so lucky to have such a relationship? Angels do walk among us and in this case the angel was a cat.

CPSIA information can be obtained
at www.ICGtesting.com
Printed in the USA
FFOW05n0037280814

9 781937 260934